Artist Ted

by Andrea Beaty and Pascal Lemaitre

MARGARET K. McELDERRY BOOKS

NEW YORK   LONDON   TORONTO   SYDNEY

To Sharon Janie with love—A. B

To the artist Slade Morrison
—P. L.

MARGARET K. McELDERRY BOOKS
An imprint of Simon & Schuster
Children's Publishing Division
1230 Avenue of the Americas
New York, New York 10020

MARGARET K. McELDERRY BOOKS
is a trademark of Simon & Schuster, Inc.
For information about special discounts
for bulk purchases, please contact Simon &
Schuster Special Sales at 1-866-506-1949 or
business@simonandschuster.com
The Simon & Schuster Speakers Bureau
can bring authors to your live event. For
more information or to book an event
contact the Simon & Schuster Speakers
Bureau at 1-866-248-3049 or visit our
website at www.simonspeakers.com
The text for this book is set in Bliss.
The illustrations for this book are rendered
in brush and ink, then colored digitally.
Manufactured in India
0411 MS
1 2 3 4 5 6 7 8 9 10
Library of Congress Cataloging-in-
Publication Data
Beaty, Andrea
Artist Ted / Andrea Beaty ;
illustrated by Pascal Lemaitre.—1st ed.
p. cm.
Summary: Ted decides that his bedroom, as
well as his school, need the touch of an artist,
and when he cannot find one, he becomes
one for the day, to the dismay of his mother,
principal, and a new classmate, Pierre.
ISBN 978-1-4169-5374-6 (hardcover)
[1. Artists—Fiction. 2. Schools—Fiction.
3. Imagination—Fiction. 4. Humorous stories.]
I. Lemaitre, Pascal, ill. II. Title
PZ7.B380547Art 2012
[E]—dc22
2010027936

FIRST
EDITION

One morning Ted woke up, got out of bed, and looked around the room. It looked the same as it did every morning.

That's not good, thought Ted. *I need an artist to spiff things up around here.*

Ted looked everywhere, but he couldn't find one.
And since Ted couldn't find an artist . . .

. . . he became an artist.

Every artist needs an imagination.

"I have one of those!" said Artist Ted, and he imagined a monkey juggling stinky socks. "Now, if only I had a paintbrush."

Artist Ted did not have a paintbrush,
so he made one.

Artist Ted didn't have any paint,
so he made some of that, too.

He looked around at the white walls and he was inspired. Artist Ted painted and painted and painted. His mother was impressed.

"What is that!?!" she asked.

"It's my masterpiece," he said. "I call it *Green*."

"It isn't green," said his mother.

"Do we have any pea soup?" asked Artist Ted.

"Go to school," said his mother.

At school Artist Ted walked down the long white hallway. He was inspired.

He painted and painted and painted.

Principal Bigham was impressed.
"What is that?!?" he asked.
"I call it *Principal Bigham*," said Artist Ted.

"I don't look like that!" said Principal Bigham,
and he turned bright red.

"A masterpiece!" said Artist Ted.
"GO TO CLASS!" said Principal Bigham.
"That's the name of my other masterpiece,"
 said Artist Ted.

Principal Bigham was speechless.
"No need to thank me," said Artist Ted.
"It's all in a day's work for a True Artiste."

Artist Ted went to Mrs. Johnson's class.
There was a new student in class.
His name was Pierre, and he was very quiet.

Pierre wore a beautiful white shirt and sat right in front of Artist Ted. Artist Ted was inspired.

He painted and painted and painted.

Pierre was not impressed. He frowned and did not speak.
"A mime!" said Artist Ted, and he waved at Pierre.

Pierre frowned even
harder and sank down
in his seat.

At lunch Artist Ted sat by Pierre. Pierre poked his
potatoes with a fork and pushed them into a big pile.
"A sculptor!" said Artist Ted, and he helped Pierre
make a masterpiece.

Pierre was not impressed. He frowned again.
He stomped his feet and jumped up and down.

"A dancer!" said Artist Ted, and he danced all
around the room.

He finished with a gigantic bow.

When he stood up, Pierre was gone.
"AN ESCAPE ARTIST!" said Artist Ted.
"Wow!"

Artist Ted looked everywhere for Pierre. Mrs. Johnson and her class looked for Pierre too. Principal Bigham ran this way and that.

"Help!" he yelled. "Call the weatherman! Call the gardener! Call the library! Just call somebody!"

But Artist Ted was already there.

He found Pierre high in the tree.
Just then, the weatherman arrived
with the gardener and the librarians.

They watched Pierre's teardrops splash onto the grass.
"At least he's not snowing," said the weatherman.

"Could he water the shrubs, too?" asked the gardener.
"Hope he doesn't get the books wet!" said the librarians.

Artist Ted looked around the playground.
He saw the white wall of the school building
and he was inspired, but he needed help!

He told Mrs. Johnson and she told her students.
They painted and painted and painted.

At last they finished.

"A work of art," said Artist Ted.

Just then, someone grabbed his paintbrush.
It was Pierre! He looked at the wall and frowned.
Pierre painted and painted and painted.

At last he finished too.
Pierre stopped frowning.

"A masterpiece!" said Artist Ted.
Pierre smiled and waved.
"You are a True Artiste,"
said Artist Ted. "Keep the brush."

That night Ted put away his paints and went
to bed knowing he had done a good job.
There are so many wonderful arts to explore,
he thought. *How could anyone try them all?*
Ted did not have a clue.

But I could get one, he thought, . . . *if I had a
magnifying glass!*